Foxglove

Field Poppy

Delphinium

Wildrose

Cornflower

Yellow Fumitory

Crow-peas

English Oak

Horse Chestnut

Blackberry

Crab Apple

Russula xerampelina

Sweet Briar rose hip

False chanterelle

Blender
98' - '99

My Way
Sally

Written by Mindy Bingham
and Penelope Colville Paine

Illustrated by Itoko Maeno

Advocacy Press, Santa Barbara

To all the 'Sallys' of the World

Text Copyright © 1988 by Melinda W. Bingham and
Penelope C. Paine
Illustration Copyright © 1988 by Itoko Maeno

 Published by Advocacy Press
P.O. Box 236
Santa Barbara, California 93102 USA

Advocacy Press is a division of Girls Incorporated of Greater Santa Barbara, an affiliate of Girls Incorporated.

Library of Congress Cataloging-in-Publication Data

Bingham, Mindy, 1950-
   My way Sally / written by Mindy Bingham and Penelope Colville Paine; illustrated by Itoko Maeno.

   Summary: A little foxhound with the potential to lead the pack at the hunt someday forms a friendship with a young fox and has an adventure in Windsor Castle that set her on a course of action for leading the hounds as they have never been led before.

   1. Foxhunds—Juvenile fiction. [1. Foxhounds—Fiction. 2. Dogs—Fiction.
3. Hunting—Fiction. 4. Windsor Castle—Fiction. 5. England—Fiction.] I. Paine,
Penelope Colville, 1946-   . II. Maeno, Itoko, ill. III. Title.
PZ10.3.B513My 1988
[Fic]—dc19   88-2653
                                                  CIP
ISBN 0-911655-27-1   AC

Printed in Hong Kong

Special thanks to Eric Ashby, Tony Collins and Julia Warman

BALOO! BALOO! BALOO! The sound of the kennelman's horn broke the silence of the early morning.

The little foxhound knew she was supposed to follow that sound and stay with the other puppies, but the excitement of her first outing was just too much.

All that could be seen were the narrow, brown and white tails of the puppies as they romped through the long, damp grass. So it was no wonder that George, the kennelman, did not notice when one of those tails disappeared over a ridge as the others followed him on through the meadow.

The puppy's curiosity had gotten the best of her, and it seemed there was a very interesting scent in a distant clump of bushes. Ignoring the horn's insistent call, she broke away to investigate.

As she approached the thicket, the bushes rustled and ...

... she came nose to nose with another young animal.

"Who are you?" the little foxhound asked as she backed up for a better look.

"I am a fox!" exclaimed the other creature. "I live in the woods. Who are you?"

"Well, I am a foxhound," replied the pup as she inched closer again.

"Hmm ... fox ... foxhound," thought the fuzzy little animal. And then with a start she leaped in the air with excitement. "I know! We must be RELATED!" she cried out. "We look somewhat alike. Maybe we're cousins ... or at least distant relatives."

And with that they bounded out of the thicket, frolicking down the hill. They ran and played and yipped.

One with a bushy tail . . . one with a thin tail.
One with a long coat . . . the other with a short coat.
One reddish . . . one with spots.

The babies did not notice the two bright eyes peering from a hole in the ground.

7

"Oh, no," thought the mother fox when she saw the dog. Her first instinct was to race out of her den, grab her kit by the neck and drag her back into the safety of the foxhole.

But then a more chilling thought crossed her mind. Would she need to be a decoy and run out to draw the pack of dogs away from her baby? Her memories of the danger of the chase were not nearly as frightening as the thought of what would happen to her babies if she did not return.

In the next instant she realized she was not watching a pack of foxhounds or the people on horses. She did not hear the hunting horns and the cries of "tallyho". All she saw were two young animals playing tag in the filtered sunshine and enjoying their new friendship.

"Felicity, come," she demanded in that special tone that made the fox kit stop instantly in her tracks. Without knowing why, the little fox immediately ran to the side of her mother. As they turned to dart away, they saw the startled look of the puppy.

Watching the two foxes retreat up the hill, the little foxhound looked around to find that she was all alone; George and the puppies were nowhere to be seen. It was at that moment the youngster realized she was lost.

She didn't know where she was and she had no idea how to get home. Just as the two foxes were about to disappear from sight, she sat down, threw back her head and cried a mournful puppy howl.

The mother fox stopped.

Her fox instinct told her to run, yet her mothering instinct would not let her. This young creature needed her help, and she could not turn her back on it. She barked at the puppy to follow her.

Leading the puppy and her kit to the highest point in the valley, the mother fox lifted her nose to the wind. Slowly she turned around and perked her large ears. Suddenly something caught her attention. "Follow me," she demanded, and rushed off through the chestnut trees.

At an opening in a low stone wall the fox stopped. "We can go no farther," the mother fox said. "Follow this footpath and go over the ridge. There you will find your home."

The little foxhound ran only a few steps before remembering she had not thanked the fox for helping her. But when she turned to say good-bye they were already gone.

A few minutes later she was racing down the hill toward George and Wendy, the owner's daughter. She was so relieved that, in her hurry, she tripped and rolled down the last part of the hill. She landed right in front of a very angry George.

11

"About time," growled George.

Wendy stooped to pet the muddy bundle at her feet. "Naughty puppy," she scolded softly. "Where have you been?"

"Sallied off again, didn't you?" grumbled George. "How am I going to train her, Miss Wendy? This dog will be useless for the hunt."

"Oh, George, don't say that," pleaded Wendy. "Why, she is the pick of the litter. You know she is very fast and quite clever. She's just a little headstrong – she likes to go her own way."

"Wrong way if you ask me, Miss," scoffed the groom. "And that's what I will call her ... Wrong Way Sally."

12

Choosing to ignore George's "wrong way"
comment, Wendy responded, "Sally is a perfect
name for her. Why, isn't 'sally' another word for
'venturing forth' or making an excursion? She's
certainly an adventurer."

"Let's hope that she is not too much of an adventurer," George said, shaking
his head. "She has a big job to learn. Your father expects her to be the leader of
the pack some day."

"The leader!" exclaimed Wendy. "Did you hear that, Sally? Father expects you
to be the leader of the hunt pack. Isn't that exciting?"

"Leader? What's a leader?" wondered Sally as she began to doze off in
Wendy's arms during the walk back to the kennels.

Through the summer and the following winter, Sally grew bigger and stronger. One morning she and her litter mates were assembled in front of the local inn. Beautiful horses with their riders in black coats milled in front as the red-coated huntsmasters gave final instructions. A pack of seasoned foxhounds eyed the new recruits.

"Morning, Miss," George greeted Wendy as she rode up on her dappled mare. "Come to watch the young dogs follow their first hunt?"

"Yes, I thought it would be fun." answered Wendy. "I especially want to see how our Sally fares today. Do you think she will try to run towards the front?"

The hunting horn sounded.

"Well, you won't have to wait long to find out, Miss Wendy," George chortled as he slapped her mare on the rump. "Off with you now, and take care of yourself."

After only a very short time, Sally sensed a rapid change in the older dogs. Their muscles tightened, their noses went to the ground, and excitement began to race through the pack. Just then the old lead dog threw back her head and howled to the other dogs and riders. At that instant Sally caught the scent, too.

Her leap forward to follow the other running dogs was stopped in mid-air. In that moment she remembered what it was that she had smelled and who it was that she was about to chase. A picture of the mother fox and her baby flashed before her eyes.

As the dogs and riders dashed off across the field, Sally could be seen running ... back to the manor house.

16

Sally didn't even greet Wendy when she finally found the dog hiding in the back of the stable. Wendy knew how she felt.

"Oh, Sally, I'm not sure I like foxhunting either," sympathized Wendy. "On the one hand I like the dogs, the horses and the crisp fall mornings. I like the color, and the challenging riding and the Hunt Ball, but ... there are other things I don't like at all."

She sat down in the hay beside the miserable dog and stroked Sally's head as she talked.

"I don't understand why we have to chase a fox," continued Wendy. "My father says that following a fox is what makes the ride exciting. The dogs and riders need something clever and fast to pursue. Because of the unpredictable way the fox runs, the riders never know which direction they will go next. This is what tests their riding skill and makes it fun. Father says that without the challenge of following the fox, the outing would be no more demanding than a canter across the countryside."

"Fox hunting is a tradition," interrupted George who had been standing in the doorway listening. "It's the way it has been done for centuries. Besides, farmers don't like foxes because they raid their hen houses. The hunters help the farmers keep the fox population low."

"George, if that is really necessary, there are more humane ways to accomplish the same thing," responded Wendy. "Anyway, most farmers don't like the damage the galloping horses do to their fields and pastures."

"Well, Missy, if you and Sally can come up with a better way to provide an exciting ride, I'm sure the huntsmaster will want to hear about it," chuckled George, shaking his head as he left the stable.

"A better way," mused Wendy. "Sally, if only there were a better way."

18

A few weeks later Wendy arranged with her father to take Sally to the Windsor Horse Show. Sally found herself in the back of the car, fascinated by the countryside racing by the window.

As they parked the car in the roundabout leading into Windsor, Wendy cried out with excitement, "Look everyone! The Royal Standard is flying! That means the Queen is staying at the castle."

Windsor was much busier than the village. There were noisy, green busses, rumbling trucks and lots of cars. People were everywhere.

On a cobblestone street in front of a row of charming shops, Wendy and her father tied Sally to a post while they went into a store. "Stay," Wendy's father commanded. "We'll be back in just a few minutes."

Sally tried to sit quietly, but she soon became bored. Suddenly, a small gray mouse darted between her paws into the shop. Sally was ready to play, so with one clever tug, she slipped from her collar and ran after the mouse.

20

At the back of the shop was a long, dark passageway, one of many used in centuries past by secret visitors entering the castle. The mouse disappeared through the bars covering its entrance. Sally followed, undaunted by the black tunnel. Her nose told her which way the mouse had gone.

Sally caught only a glimpse of the mouse as it slipped into a tiny hole at the top of the staircase. Knowing she was too big to follow it, she gave up and stopped to catch her breath.

But what she saw when she turned around took her breath away. She was standing in the most beautiful room she had ever seen. There were twinkling crystal lights, beautifully carved ceilings, exquisite gold furniture and a magnificent marble fireplace. On the walls were large paintings of what appeared to be very important people. One of them looked a lot like the woman on the sign post at the Queen's Head Inn.

As Sally walked over to get a better look, a guard rounded a corner of the room. Spotting the dog, he shouted at her to stop. Startled, Sally turned and ran out of the room. The guard blew his whistle and then ran after her.

Now it was Sally's turn to be pursued.

Before she knew it, more people joined in the chase. She was terrified. "What will they do with me when they catch me?" she thought. Awful pictures raced through her mind.

24

She ran from one room to the next. In each room there were more people waiting to grab her.

The terror was almost more than she could stand. "Was this how the fox felt?" Sally thought as she frantically looked for an escape.

By now it seemed that everyone in the whole world was after Sally. She slipped and skidded across the floors and carpets. Shouting could be heard from all directions.

Her heart was pounding and her legs were growing tired. She didn't know how much longer she could continue to run. "Think, Sally, think!" she cried to herself. "You must outwit them."

And that's just what she did! No one noticed her as they charged past.

Seeing her chance to escape, Sally raced outdoors. Slipping under a boxwood bush, tired and frightened, she tried to catch her breath. But before she could even think about what to do next, she was startled by . . .

... two very different looking dogs.

"Who are you?" demanded one of the dogs.

"And what's more," added the other, "how did you get here?"

Sensing that she needed to impress these rather haughty dogs, Sally gathered her courage and sat up as tall as she could.

"I am Sally, a foxhound, and ... "

The largest Corgi interrupted, "I am Prudence and this is Hattie. We are Her Majesty, the Queen's Corgis."

Sally looked puzzled. "What is the Queen?" she asked innocently. "I've seen her picture, her flag and her inn. She must be very important."

The Corgis were amused. "The Queen, my dear," answered Hattie, "is Britain's monarch. She is the head of state." And then, sensing that Sally still did not understand, she continued ... "She is a leader!"

"Like the leader of the pack?" Sally asked, still puzzled.

"Almost," they giggled as they winked at each other. "With her ministers she makes important decisions about which way to go with ...

"Catch that foxhound!" cried the guard as the stream of people burst into the garden.

Sally turned to run ...

… and ran right into the Queen and her Minister.

"Pardon me, Your Majesty," panted the guard as he stiffened to a salute. "What a chase we've had trying to catch this little rascal. Dare I say it, Ma'am, but she almost outfoxed us. I'd better get her off to the police station straight away."

The Minister looked down at the cowering dog. "Quite right. Strange dogs are not allowed in Windsor Castle," he agreed. "Regulations, and all that … it's off to the police station with you."

"One minute, Mr. Wallington," commanded the Queen. "Let's not be too hasty. This dog seems harmless, and I'm sure her owner is looking for her. I do not think it would serve any purpose to punish her – such measures hardly seem necessary. Let the dogs play for awhile, and I will ask a guard to walk her to the front gate to find her owners."

The dogs ran off for a last romp.

"Goodness, what a narrow escape," panted Sally. "I thought it was curtains for me."

"If it hadn't been for the Queen," responded Prudence, "it might have been."

"Before I was so rudely interrupted, I was trying to explain what a leader is," asserted Hattie. "When you are the leader, everyone looks to you for direction, and you decide which way to go."

"And lucky you!" Prudence chortled. "This leader decided that you will go free today."

"How do you become a leader?" asked Sally.

"Well, first, you have to be pretty clever," responded Hattie. "Then you have to study, practice and work hard to gain the respect and confidence of those who must follow you. But once you are the leader, you usually make the rules."

The Queen beckoned to the dogs and summoned the guard. "Come along now. We've had a call from the front gate, and your owners are there waiting."

"Thank you," said Sally to the Corgis as she was ushered out.

"Our pleasure, my dear," the two dogs called after her. "Next time make sure you know where you are going."

The words of the Corgis spun in her head as she walked to the front gate of Windsor Castle. Now she knew which way she must go.

From that day on there was no stopping Sally. She returned to the manor and began her training in earnest. Throughout the late spring and early summer, George noticed that Sally's attitude toward her job had changed. Whenever the young pack of dogs was taken out for a drill, Sally would practice her bay until she was the loudest and clearest.

... refine her sense of smell until she could pick up and follow any scent no matter where it was.

... exercise until she developed into the swiftest dog in the pack.

Finally, through her talents and training, she began to command the respect of the other hounds, and they began to follow her.

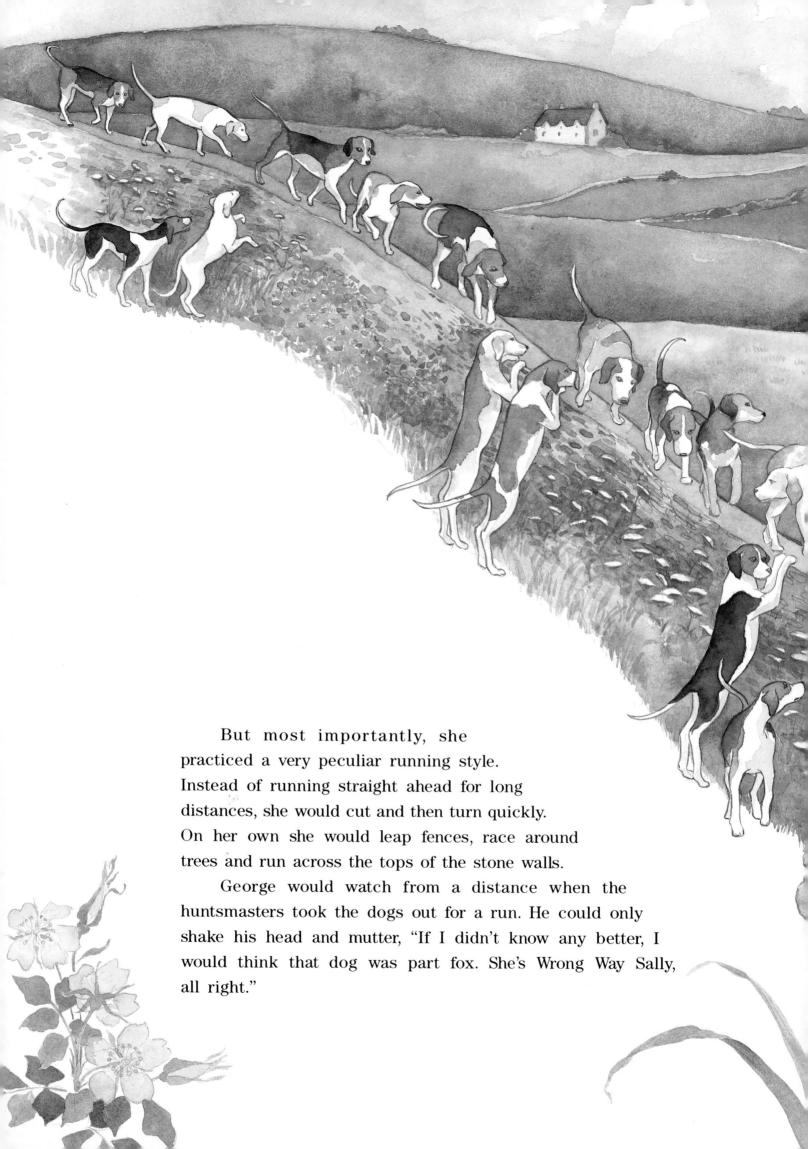

But most importantly, she
practiced a very peculiar running style.
Instead of running straight ahead for long
distances, she would cut and then turn quickly.
On her own she would leap fences, race around
trees and run across the tops of the stone walls.

George would watch from a distance when the
huntsmasters took the dogs out for a run. He could only
shake his head and mutter, "If I didn't know any better, I
would think that dog was part fox. She's Wrong Way Sally,
all right."

On the morning of the first hunt of the season, Sally found it hard to contain her excitement. Because of her hard work and practice, she had been chosen leader of the pack. She knew this was her chance to put her plan into action.

As the dogs and horses trotted down the road and over the glen, Sally kept her nose to the ground. It was not long before she found what she was searching for ... the scent of a fox. Raising her voice in her hound howl, Sally signaled the hunt to begin.

"Tallyho!" cried the huntsmasters. BALOO, BALOO, BALOO warned the hunting horn. The horses leaped forward into a gallop to follow the pack of dogs in full cry.

As the riders and hounds raced across the field leading up to the woods, a lone fox could be seen running frantically ...

in the opposite direction!

"I don't believe it!" shouted George."Wrong Way Sally has done it again."

The quiet of the valley was broken with sounds of the melodic chorus of baying hounds and the thundering hooves of twenty horses. From their vantage point on the highest hill in the valley, George and Wendy watched as the hunt went over stone walls, down the sides of the riverbank, across open fields and in and out of the trees and across fences. It was one of the most thrilling rides they had ever seen.

44

Wendy finally turned to George and said, "Wrong Way ... I don't think so." And then, with the kind of twinkle in her eye that comes with finally figuring out a puzzle, she added, "I think we need to call her My Way Sally. Just look at the course Sally is leading. It is quite deliberate. The hunters will never know they are not following a fox. And see – everyone is having a jolly good time."

Yes, everyone had a great time that day ...

even the fox!

Dear Parents and Educators,

Today the opportunities for leadership roles in our society are opening up to women. Yet it seems that if we are to encourage young women to strive for positions of leadership, we must first show them that power can be a means to accomplish goals that reflect their personal values . . . not an end in itself. That is why we wrote **My Way Sally.**

> **Today:**
>
> **Only 14.7% of our legislators are women.**
>
> **Only 1.7% of the corporate officers of _Fortune_ 500 companies are women.**
>
> **Only 4% of the top management in society's major institutions are women.**

This is unfortunate for us all. A recent study by the Center for Creative Leadership concludes that executive women are more likely than executive men to move in new and original directions. In a world perilously close to extinction, new directions and leadership styles are desperately needed. We can no longer afford to believe that to have "winners" we must have "losers." We can no longer afford a culture based on rugged individualism and ruthless competition.

Women's responsibility for nurturing life has endowed them with a value system that promotes compassion, co-operation and connectedness. They find the vision of a non-violent, non-racist world where problems are negotiated to "win-win" solutions irresistible. As "outsiders" who did not make the rules, they are not chained to tradition. Therefore, they are more likely to introduce new enlightened and socially responsible solutions. However, women must first be motivated to strive for leadership . . . to assume the proportion of power to which their numbers entitle them.

For a young woman to strive for a position of power, she must first view power as a positive force. Unfortunately, from early childhood our children tend to connect power with control and domination. From video games to movies, from literature to the evening news, they have seen power as manipulative, impassioned, dangerous, and uncontrolled. It is no wonder that few women aspire to leadership roles.

Studies consistently show that the career characteristic most appealing to young females is _the opportunity to help others._ This is the key. If girls are to commit the energy and accept the sacrifices required to reach the top of the power structure, we must help them make an early connection between leadership and the ability to change the rules, and set new directions required to create a saner, safer, and more humane world.

Here's what you can do!

Encourage your daughters to want, and then seek, leadership responsibilities. Encourage your sons to accept and pursue leadership styles based on co-operation, negotiation and "win/win" solutions.

Discuss the positive uses of power with your children. Identify leaders within your community who are finding innovative solutions to long-time problems.

Encourage calculated risk taking and independent thinking. Reward creativity and innovation. Teach your children to accept and learn from criticism; if they fail, to pick themselves up and try again.

When a leadership opportunity presents itself at school, at church or in the community, support your children's participation.

Discuss current world events and ask your children how they would deal with them if they were the leader. Brainstorm and analyze "win/win" solutions.

Review school curriculum and make sure that powerful women in history are studied as well as men.

Ask older students to analyze the leadership styles of the truly great leaders in history. Can they identify a "_Sally_"?

About the Authors

Since 1973 Mindy Bingham has been the Executive Director of the Girls Club of Santa Barbara, California. Coauthor of seven other books including the best seller: ***Choices: A Teen Woman's Journal for Self-awareness and Personal Planning***, and the acclaimed children's book ***Minou***, she is especially interested in writing on equity issues for girls and young women.

Born in London, Penelope Colville Paine received her degree from the University of London, Goldsmiths' College. A California resident since 1972, she has worked for Girls Clubs for twelve years. She helped develop the series of life-planning journals that includes ***Choices***. Now she travels extensively throughout the United States as a speaker on early equity and career planning issues.

About the Illustrator

Itoko Maeno was born in Tokyo, where she studied at Tama College of Art. Her art has appeared in many books including ***Minou***. Itoko is accomplished in a wide range of styles, but she is best known for her delicate and intricate water colors. She spent three weeks in the English countryside sketching in preparation for ***My Way Sally***.

Illustrated Children's Books by Advocacy Press

Berta Benz and the Motorwagen
Father Gander Nursery Rhymes
Kylie's Song
Mimi Makes a Splash
Mimi Takes Charge
Minou
Mother Nature Nursery Rhymes
My Way Sally
Nature's Wonderful World in Rhyme
Time for Horatio
Tonia the Tree

Journal/Workbooks for Self-awareness & Personal Planning

Choices: A Teen Woman's Journal for Self-awareness
  and Personal Planning
Challenges: A Young Man's Journal for Self-awareness
  and Personal Planning
More Choices: A Strategic Planning Guide for Mixing
  Career and Family
Changes: A Woman's Journal for Self-awareness and
  Personal Planning

You can find these books at better bookstores.
Or you may send for a free catalog from Advocacy Press,
P.O. Box 236, Santa Barbara, California 93102

Daffodil

Crab Apple

Forget-me-not

Bluebell

Dead-nettle

Violet

Buttercup

Holly

Mistletoe

Cedar

Snowdrop

Old Man's Beard